MW01012642

Disney
DUMBO

Read-Along
STORYBOOK AND CD

Find out how little Dumbo uses his big ears to soar to fame and become the world's one and only flying elephant! You can read along with me in your book. You'll know it's time to turn the page when you hear this sound. . . . **Let's begin now**.

First Paperback Edition, February 2019

1 3 5 7 9 10 8 6 4 2

Library of Congress Control Number: 2018955236

ISBN 978-1-4231-4379-6   FAC-038091-18355

Printed in the United States of America

For more Disney Press fun, visit www.disneybooks.com

SUSTAINABLE FORESTRY INITIATIVE   Certified Sourcing
www.sfiprogram.org
SFI-00993
Logo Applies to Text Stock Only

Disney PRESS
Los Angeles • New York

Early one morning, a flock of storks flew across the sky. In their beaks they carried precious bundles over a big circus. At just the right moment, the storks released their special deliveries, sending them gently floating down to the circus tents below.

From her pen, Mrs. Jumbo watched the bundles drop softly to the ground. Surely one of them held her own little baby, she thought. She saw a baby kangaroo, a fuzzy little bear cub, and a long-necked baby giraffe. But no special bundle came for Mrs. Jumbo.

As the animals boarded the circus train the next morning, Mrs. Jumbo searched the sky again, but there wasn't a stork in sight.

The Ringmaster was ready to go.

Casey Jr. whistled and, with a powerful tug, headed down the track. The circus was on its way once again.

Mr. Stork was running very late with his delivery. When he spotted the circus train below, he quickly flew down and landed on the roof of a train car. "Mrs. Jumbo! Calling Mrs. Jumbo. Oh, where's that Mrs. Jumbo?"

From one of the cars, he spotted some elephant trunks waving at him.

Mr. Stork hopped into the train car. "Which one of you ladies is expecting?"

The elephants excitedly pointed to Mrs. Jumbo.

Mrs. Jumbo smiled shyly as Mr. Stork placed the bundle at her feet. "Here is a baby with eyes of blue, straight from heaven, right to you! Or . . . Straight from heaven, up above, here is a baby for you to love!"

Mrs. Jumbo eagerly untied the bundle with her trunk to uncover an adorable baby elephant with a sweet little face and big blue eyes.

The other elephants smiled adoringly at the little baby. "Oh, he *is* cute, isn't he?"

When they asked Mrs. Jumbo what she would call him, she looked down with pride at her little one and told them his name: Jumbo Junior.

Suddenly, the baby elephant sneezed.

His ears, which had been neatly tucked behind his head, flopped open . . . and they were enormous!

The other elephants shrieked with laughter at the sight of him.

"Just look at those—those E-A-R-S!"

Mrs. Jumbo glared back at them. But the elephants just turned up their trunks at her and her little Jumbo Junior.

They even came up with a nickname for him. "Jumbo? You mean Dumbo!"

Angry at the teasing from the other elephants, Mrs. Jumbo whisked her baby away. She didn't care if her baby's ears were big. She thought he was beautiful just the way he was. As she gently cradled him in her trunk, Dumbo smiled, feeling safe and warm with his mother.

The next day, the townspeople followed the parade to
the circus grounds. Inside the circus tent, Mrs. Jumbo was
quietly bathing Dumbo when a bunch of rowdy boys ran in.
As soon as they spotted Dumbo and his oversized ears,
they began to make fun of the little elephant.

Laughing and jeering, they crawled beneath the ropes and pulled his ears! Dumbo tried to hide behind his mother. Mrs. Jumbo trumpeted angrily, but the boys still wouldn't leave him alone. So Mrs. Jumbo picked up a bale of straw and threw it at the boys to scare them away.

Hearing the boys' yells, the Ringmaster ran into the tent to see about the commotion.

He ordered his men to capture Mrs. Jumbo. And then the Ringmaster took little Dumbo from her.

The Ringmaster had his men lock poor Mrs. Jumbo in a wagon apart from the rest of the circus. Dumbo's mother was so worried about her little one. All she could think about was cradling him close to her again.

Little Dumbo cried for his mother. But the other elephants turned their backs on him. He felt like he didn't have a friend in the world . . . until a little mouse named Timothy noticed him. "Poor little guy." Timothy shook his head. "What's the matter with his ears? I think they're cute." And without thinking twice, Timothy decided to help Dumbo.

Timothy introduced himself to the little elephant. "Hello, Dumbo. I'm your friend."

Dumbo smiled shyly at Timothy.

Then the tiny mouse asked Dumbo if he might like to hear his plan to free Mrs. Jumbo.

Dumbo nodded, listening closely to his new friend.

"All we gotta do is make you a star. A headliner! Dumbo the Great!"

The next day, Timothy was ready to put his plan in action. He tied up Dumbo's ears to keep them out of the way. The Ringmaster blew his whistle, and the elephants began to make a pyramid. The crowd watched with wonder as the elephant pyramid rose higher and higher until it nearly reached the top of the circus tent.

Then the Ringmaster announced that Dumbo, the world's smallest little elephant, would spring to the very top of the pyramid!

Dumbo dashed into the ring. But before he could make his leap, his ears came untied, sending him crashing into the elephant pyramid!

For a moment, the crowd watched as the elephants swayed to the left, then to the right. Then, trumpeting and bellowing, the elephants began to tumble, sending the crowds running!

As the elephants fell, they hit the poles that were holding the tent up. There was a loud crack as the center pole snapped in two. The big top began to fall, and with a loud whoosh, the giant tent collapsed.

The other elephants blamed Dumbo for what had happened, turning their backs on him once again.

So Dumbo joined the clowns' firefighting act. For the act, they dressed Dumbo up as a baby, put him high up in a building surrounded by make-believe flames, and then made him jump into a bucket of foam far below. The crowds laughed and laughed at the act, but poor Dumbo felt humiliated, hurt, and miserable.

After the show, Timothy scrubbed his friend's sad little face. "You were stupendous! You oughta be proud!"

But his friend's kind words couldn't stop Dumbo's tears.

Timothy thought for a second. "Dumbo, I forgot to tell ya! We're going over to see your mother. Come on!"

A hopeful smile crossed Dumbo's face at the thought of seeing his mother.

Later that night, while the circus folk slept, Timothy took Dumbo to the wagon where his mother was chained up.

"Mrs. Jumbo, someone to see ya!"

Mrs. Jumbo was overjoyed to see her baby. She put her trunk through the bars of the window and rocked her little Dumbo, making him feel warm and safe and loved.

The next day, Dumbo was filled with dread as he climbed to the top of the building once again. Timothy wanted more than anything to give Dumbo confidence. Suddenly, an idea came to him. Timothy handed him a feather, telling him it was a magic feather that would help him fly.

Could it be true? Dumbo wondered. But he trusted Timothy. So holding the magic feather tight, Dumbo jumped.

At first, Dumbo and Timothy soared through the air. But halfway down, Dumbo lost the feather! Without it, he thought he couldn't fly. As they plummeted toward the ground, Timothy quickly told Dumbo the feather wasn't really magic. He didn't need it to fly. All he had to do was believe in himself.

"Dumbo! Open them ears! Come on, fly!"

Whoosh! Dumbo opened his ears just before he hit the ground. The clowns, the Ringmaster, and the audience watched in amazement as Dumbo flew up, down, and all around the big top. He was a flying elephant!

Then Dumbo began to play. He chased the clowns and shot peanuts at the mean elephants.

Timothy shouted for joy. "Whee! We did it! You're making history!"

In the days that followed, Dumbo became the most famous elephant in the world, and people came from all over to see the little elephant with the big ears fly. Timothy, who was now Dumbo's manager, became famous, too.

The Ringmaster freed Mrs. Jumbo and gave her and Dumbo a fancy car at the end of the circus train. And even though Dumbo was a star now, there was nothing more wonderful than being with his mother again. When she hugged him close, he was the happiest little elephant in the whole world.

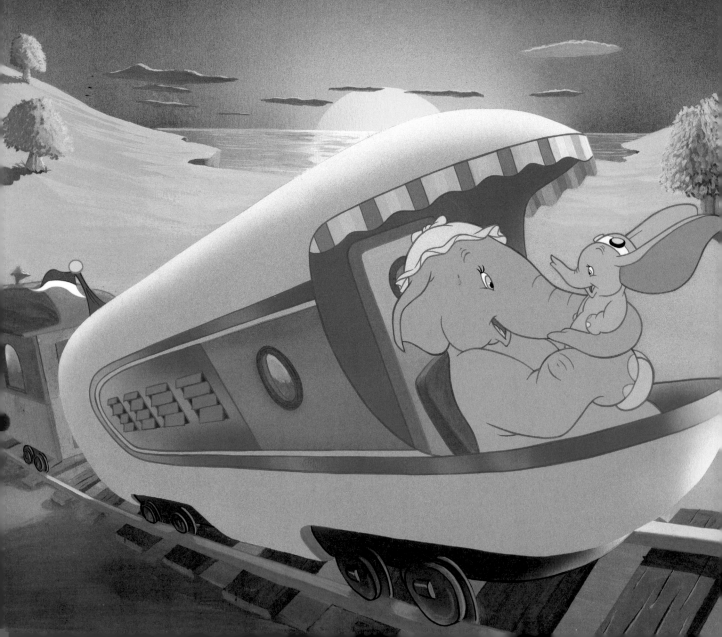